Animal Antics

THE SINGING SHEEP

LUCY COURTENAY

Illustrated by Phil Alderson

stripes

Animals!

Everyone loves animals. Feathery, furry, fierce. Scaly, scary, hairy. Cute, a bit smelly, all-round bonkers.

But let's be honest. How well do we really know them?
I know my dog, you might say.
I know my cat and my hamster.

Ah, I say. You may think you know them, but you DON'T.
When you watch them, they do catty
and doggy and hamstery things.
But what about when you're not watching?
Who knows what they do when you're snoozing
in your beds or when you're at school?

This book is the property of

**Haberdashers' Aske's
School for Girls**

Infant Library Bus

In memory of Caron – LC

For Betsy – PA

STRIPES PUBLISHING
An imprint of Magi Publications
1 The Coda Centre, 189 Munster Road,
London SW6 6AW

A paperback original
First published in Great Britain in 2011

Text copyright © Lucy Courtenay, 2011
Illustrations copyright © Phil Alderson, 2011

ISBN: 978-1-84715-158-2

The right of Lucy Courtenay and Phil Alderson to
be identified as the author and illustrator of this work
respectively has been asserted by them in accordance
with the Copyright, Designs and Patents Act, 1988.

Printed and bound in the UK.

10 9 8 7 6 5 4 3 2 1

And what about the rest of the animal kingdom?
The world is full of amazing creatures –
from camels in the desert, to baboons
in the forest, and fish in the deepest ocean.

We know even less about them.
For all we know, they might like dancing. Or doing
handstands. Or playing thumb wars. Actually, not that
one because most animals don't have thumbs.
But you know what I mean.

Maybe we don't know animals as well as we think.
Take **SHEEP,** for instance…

Chapter One

It was a quiet day on Woolly Farm. The sun
shone lazily. The breeze blew gustily. The birds
sang, then stopped because their voices
sounded a bit loud.

"Ah," said Sir Simon the prize ram, resting
his horns on his fleecy back and breathing
deeply. "There's nothing like peace and quiet,
is there, ladies?"

"Mmm," agreed the flock. "Lovely, Sir Simon."

"Just the way it should be," said Serafina, the oldest ewe. "Just us and our thoughts."

"And some grass," added a younger sheep with very shiny hooves.

"Quite so, Sadie," said Serafina. "Us, our thoughts and some grass."

Down in the lane there was a rumble as Farmer Woolly's truck came into view.

"Farmer Woolly needs to check his engine," Serafina said, with a flick of her ears. "There's a sort of … extra noise about it today."

There was indeed an extra noise. But it was coming from inside the container on the back of the truck, not the truck itself.

"I'm … yeah … Sunny, whoo! I'm … well … funny, whoo! I … like … honey, whoo! Oh, hang on – I've never eaten honey…"

Animal Antics

"What on earth is in the back of Farmer Woolly's truck?" Serafina said, wrinkling her nose as Sir Simon trotted away.

"Life's … a … riot, yeah! Grass … my … diet, yeah! Who … needs … quiet, yeah!"

The noise was getting louder. Farmer Woolly turned into the farmyard, switched off the engine, walked round to the back of the truck and put the ramp down. The racket was now deafening.

"I'm … not … lazy, whoo! I'm … well … crazy, whoo! My name … ain't … Daisy, whoo!"

A fluffy white sheep clattered down the ramp and into the farmyard. She did a little jump, clicked her hooves and spun round in a circle.

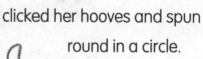

Animal Antics

"Farmer Woolly's been to market and bought *that*?" said Serafina.

"Sunny by name and Sunny by nature!" Sunny whooped. "I wanna love ya, don't wanna hate-cha! Party on, my new friends! Respect!"

The flock goggled. They'd never seen or heard a sheep this loud before.

"Girls," Serafina said in an awful voice. "You know what to do. One, two ... THREE."

The entire flock turned their backs on Sunny. She blinked at the row of woolly bottoms. It wasn't the welcome she had been expecting.

Farmer Woolly opened the gate, and Sunny trotted through it into the field. He then fastened the gate shut behind her and headed for the farmhouse.

"Hiya!" Sunny said enthusiastically.

The flock's bottoms stayed where they were.

"I'm Sunny!"

Sadie glanced round at Sunny and gave her a timid smile. So did one or two of the other young sheep. But Serafina stamped her hoof, and they quickly turned round again.

Sunny stared a little desperately at the rumps in front of her.

"You all have very nice bums!" she said at last.

"Well!" muttered an elderly ewe.

Animal Antics

"Honestly!" said another.

"No manners at all," said Serafina grimly.

"Come along, girls. We have grass to eat."

And the flock walked away, leaving Sunny alone by the gate.

Chapter Two

After the jolly chaos of Lively Farm where
Sunny had been born, Woolly Farm was a
terrible shock. Sunny tried cracking jokes.
She tried dancing. But no matter what she did,
no one in the flock seemed to like her or enjoy
talking to her. Sunny missed chatting to her
friends. She missed fun and games, and –
well, everything.

Animal Antics

"I'm bored," Sunny said loudly, one wet day in the bottom field. Rain dripped from the end of her nose, giving her an extra-miserable look.

"Why don't you eat some grass?" said Sadie.

"A sheep who's tired of grass is tired of life," said Sir Simon pompously. Raindrops shimmered on the ends of his horns.

But Sunny *was* tired of grass. She'd eaten enough to last all day, and it was barely lunchtime. She stared at the ground and wished with all her heart that something interesting would happen. Something. ANYTHING.

She looked up as Dawson the sheepdog trotted through the gate at Farmer Woolly's heels. Dawson was a border collie. His shaggy black and white coat was wet from the rain and hung in curly tendrils down his body. Raindrops dripped from the end of his nose too. He wasn't in a good mood.

Animal Antics

To be honest, Dawson was *never* in a good mood. He snarled and bit at the sheep's heels, and showed his teeth a lot. Sunny wondered if he hated all sheep, or just the sheep of Woolly Farm. If it was Woolly Farm that was getting him down, she knew how he felt.

"We're moving you lot to the top field," Dawson barked. "The bottom field is too wet. You're a soggy lot at the best of times, so it's all the same to me. But Farmer Woolly doesn't like foot rot."

"Foot rot!" the sheep said in alarm.

"Ew!" said Sadie.

Sunny wanted to cheer. At last, they were doing something different! "Cool!" she said happily, earning a sharp glance from Serafina.

"Enough chit-chat," Dawson said. "Get moving."

"I'm going behind Serafina!" said Sadie. There was less chance that Sadie would have to walk through poo and mess up her shiny hooves if she was near the front.

"I'll walk in the middle," said Suzelle. Suzelle was very proud of her curly, cream-coloured fleece, and walking in the middle of the flock was the best way to keep it from getting splashed.

"No way am I walking behind Suzelle," said Sindy, who had a thin fleece and rather a sad face. "She's got bottom problems."

"I have not got bottom problems," said Suzelle, as the other sheep giggled.

"You have."

"Have not!"

"Hurry up you daft woolly balls, or I'll bite you all," Dawson snapped.

Humming, Sunny waited for everyone else

to walk out of the bottom field ahead of her.
She didn't want to be in the front or the middle
of the flock. She wanted some space and
freedom at the back, where no one could
glare at her or tell her to be quiet.

When everyone was out of the gate, the
sheep started trotting up Woolly Farm Lane.
Farmer Woolly blew his whistle every now and
again, and Dawson crouched and snarled
and ran up and down. At the back, Sunny
watched the flock's swaying rumps and
listened to the rhythm of their trotting hooves.
Clip … clop. Clip … clop.

The further up the lane the sheep went, the
more rhythmic their hooves became. *Clip …
clop. Clip … clop.* Sunny started making up
noises to fit in between the clips and the clops.

Clip…

"Diddle-iddle-iddle—"

Animal Antics

Clop.

"Pow!"

Clip…

"Diddle-iddle-iddle—"

Clop.

"Pow!"

Next, Sunny experimented with her hooves, tapping the road in a different rhythm.

Animal Antics

Clip…
"Diddle-iddle-iddle—"
Clop.
Clippy-clip— "Pow!"
Clip…
"Diddle-iddle-iddle—"
Clop.
Clippy-clip— "Pow!"

Sunny changed her diddle-iddles to doddle-oddles. Then she changed her clippy-clips to cloppy-clops, then clippy-clops, then cloppy-clips, then clippy-clippies. Then she added a few puddle effects.

Clip went the Woolly Farm flock up ahead. They hadn't noticed Sunny's antics. *Clop.*

"Diddle-oddle-diddle oh," *clippy-splash,* "yeah!" went Sunny.

She was so pleased with the sounds she was making that she gave a little skip as the flock turned into the top field.

I'm going to call it bleat-boxing, she thought to herself. *It's time this sheep had some FUN!*

Chapter Three

Sunny splashed in the puddles and sang and tapped her hooves against the drinking trough by the gate in the top field. It rang like a bell.

Ting, ting, ting!

"Oh, yeah—"

Splashy-splash…

"So cool…"

Ting, ting, ting!

"My coat—"

Splashy-splash…

"Is wool…"

"She's so LOUD," said a sheep called Sue, who had a limp and a whiskery nose.

"It isn't even music," agreed Sue's friend Sandra, whose fleece was grey with age.

"I can barely hear the birds these days," said Serafina with a sniff.

Sunny took herself off to the top of the field and practised drumming her hooves on the trunk of a large oak tree instead.

"Baa, baa, baa…" went the flock peacefully.

Drumma-drumma-drumma-drumma-drumma went Sunny's hooves.

"Baa, baa, baa…"

Drumma-drumma drum drum.

Sindy, Suzelle and Sadie all moved up the field to see what Sunny was up to.

Animal Antics

"Hiya!" called Sunny, excited to see them. "Come to join in?"

"What are you doing?" Sadie asked.

"Bleat-boxing," Sunny said. *Drumma-drumma-drumma drum*— "Pow! Cool, isn't it? You stand up against this tree and use your hooves to make noises. Give it a try!"

Sadie stared at the damp, mossy, mushroom-covered oak tree. Then she looked at her shiny hooves. Sindy and Suzelle looked unsure as well.

"It's only moss," Sunny said. "And OK, maybe some mushrooms and lichen and stuff. But you can just wash your hooves in the trough afterwards."

"I think I'll go and eat some grass," Sadie said.

"Me too," said Sindy.

"Me three," said Suzelle.

"Mind the cowpats," Sunny said sadly, as the three young sheep headed back down the field again.

She turned back to the tree trunk and started adding some lyrics to her bleat-boxing.

"Sadie…"

Drumma-drumma-drumma drum—

"Oh, Sadie…"

Drumma-drumma drum drum.

"Her hooves are…"

Drumma-drumma-drumma drum—

"Well tidy…"

Drumma-drumma drum drum.

"Sindy…"

Drumma-drumma-drumma drum—

"Oh, Sindy…"

Drumma-drumma drum drum.

"Thinks Suzelle…"

Drumma-drumma-drumma drum—

"Is windy…"

"Can I have your attention, ladies?" Sir Simon bleated importantly. He was standing proudly on top of a hay bale in the middle of the field.

Sunny tore herself away from the oak tree and trotted down the field to hear what the old ram had to say.

"May I say how very woolly you all look today?" said Sir Simon, when everyone had gathered round. "Or should I say *ewe*. Ha ha!"

Animal Antics

All the sheep laughed at Sir Simon's terrible joke. Sunny smiled politely.

"Word has reached me," said Sir Simon, when the laughing had stopped, "about the prestigious Sheep Choir of the Year competition. As usual, Woolly Farm will be entering."

Sunny blinked in surprise. Woolly Farm was entering a *competition*?

"As you all know," Sir Simon continued, "this takes place every year at the Haybury Fleece Fair on Haybury Farm." He had clearly forgotten that Sunny was new and didn't look in her direction. "The Fleece Fair is just three weeks away, and I have now had word of the song that everyone will sing. It's a splendid piece. Sir Stanley of Mudford Farm mentioned it when we competed for the Mudford Pedigree Ram Rosette yesterday. Which I won," he added meaningfully.

"Bravo, Sir Simon!" the ewes gasped.

"But never mind about that," Sir Simon said, as if the ewes had been the ones to mention the Mudford Pedigree Ram Rosette in the first place. "The song…"

Sunny was suddenly eager to hear the song title. "The Funky Flock"? "The Sheep Shimmy"? She imagined the competition:

sheep cheering on all sides, noise and excitement everywhere. The idea was so completely wonderful that she hardly dared to picture it.

"…is called 'Sheep Are Nice'," said Sir Simon. "And it goes like this."

He tilted his head, resting his magnificent horns on his back, opened his mouth and began to sing.

SHEEP ARE NICE,
SHEEP ARE SWEET,
SHEEP GROW WOOL,
SHEEP GO BLEAT.
SHEEP ARE ALL
QUIET AS MICE,
SHEEP ARE GREAT,
SHEEP ARE NIIIICE.

Animal Antics

Everyone cheered. A few ewes were so overcome that they lay down in the damp grass for a bit.

"Well sung, Sir Simon!"

"Marvellous!"

"It's a shame that we rams don't enter," Sir Simon said, nodding his head modestly. "The Haybury Fleece Fair clashes with the annual Rutley Ram Regatta. But I shall be with you all in spirit. Or should I say *ewe* all. Ha ha!"

The flock laughed just as much at Sir Simon's ewe joke as they had the first time he'd cracked it.

Sheep Are Nice? Sunny thought with dismay. With all the songs and all the words in the world, they'd ended up with something called "Sheep Are Nice"? It had no rhythm. It had no decent tune.

Typical!

Chapter Four

"You mean, you've never heard of Sheep Choir of the Year?" said Sadie in amazement.

"We didn't enter at Lively Farm," Sunny said.

"I've only been to one," Sadie replied. "But it's brilliant! They shear us and everything!"

Sadie sounded more excited about the shearing than the competition.

"What about the singing bit?" Sunny asked.

"All the sheep choirs sing the same song," said Sadie. "We have three weeks to learn it, and then we perform it while we're completing the course for the Haybury Herding Trophy."

"Who's the judge?" Sunny asked.

"Balthasar, the Haybury Farm prize bull," said Sadie. "Of course, the humans think the Haybury Fleece Fair is just about shearing and pedigree sheep classes and the Haybury Herding Trophy." She giggled. "Aren't humans funny?"

"Hilarious," Sunny agreed. "Has Woolly Farm ever won Sheep Choir of the Year?"

"Never," said Sadie. "We've never won the Haybury Herding Trophy either. We never win anything. That's why Dawson's always so grumpy."

"So when do we start practising, er, 'Sheep Are Nice'?" asked Sunny.

"This afternoon, I expect," said Sadie. "As soon as we know what song we've got to sing, Serafina makes us practise it every day."

Serafina called the first choir practice that afternoon by the big oak tree. The spring sunshine was bright, and the top field was covered in flowers. The flock clustered beneath the shade of the tree. Sunny hung back, enjoying the sun on her woolly coat and the sweet smell of the clover flowers under her hooves. She started humming a funky little tune she'd just made up, but stopped when Serafina fixed her with a scary look.

"Before we begin," Serafina said, "may I just say again how beautifully you sang 'Sheep Are Nice' this morning, Sir Simon?"

"Thank you, Serafina," said Sir Simon, with

a twinkle. "Or should I say thank *ewe*. Ha ha!"

Sir Simon's joke wasn't getting any funnier, but the flock laughed just the same. At the back of the group, Sunny sighed. The only good thing she could see about "Sheep Are Nice" was that it was easy.

"We shall try to make you proud, Sir Simon," said Serafina. "Now, after me, choir. Exactly as we heard Sir Simon sing it. *Sheep ... Are ... Nice*," she sang in a voice nearly as deep and booming as Sir Simon's.

"*Sheep ... Are ... Nice*," the flock sang.

"*Sheep ... Have ... Lice*," Sunny sang naughtily.

Serafina stopped the song. "Is there a problem, Sunny?" she asked.

"No, Serafina," Sunny said, trying not to giggle.

"Hmm," Serafina said, frowning down

her long nose. Then she turned back to the rest of the sheep. "Let's press on, girls. *Sheep … Are … Sweet.*"

"*Sheep … Are … Sweet,*" chorused the flock.

"*They have smelly feet,*" Sunny sang.

Serafina stopped the song again.

"If you don't want to sing it properly, Sunny, perhaps you shouldn't sing it at all," she said. "And then we'll make sure Farmer Woolly leaves you behind when we all go to the Haybury Fleece Fair. Would you like that?"

Sunny couldn't imagine how Serafina would stop her getting on the truck with the rest of the sheep, but she had a feeling the old ewe would find a way.

"Well?" Serafina said.

"But it's a really boring song," Sunny said. "Can't we make it more interesting?"

Serafina gasped. Sir Simon stopped shining his horns on the grass.

"You know," said Sunny in a hopeful sort of way. "Make it fun. Give it a beat."

"A *beat*?" Serafina repeated, as if she'd never heard the word before.

Sunny gazed at the flock. The flock gazed

back at her. They didn't have a clue what she was talking about.

"Forget it," she said sadly.

"As you were, choir," said Serafina, turning back to the others. "*Sheep … Make … Wool…*"

This song is terri-ble, thought Sunny. But she didn't sing it out loud.

Chapter Five

Sunny went to all the choir rehearsals, but she
stayed at the back of the flock and sang as
little as she could. Every now and then she
spiced up "Sheep Are Nice" with a sprinkling of
silly words. Serafina lost her temper more than
once. "For the last time, it is *Sheep Are Nice* not
Sheep Have Lice, Sunny! What are you doing,
mumbling at the grass?"

"You're spoiling it for everyone, Sunny,"
Sadie said, at the end of a week of rehearsals.

"We need these rehearsals!" said Sindy.

"You have to try harder," said Suzelle. Her
coat was looking good today, as curly as a
cloud and almost as white. Sunny caught
Sindy looking enviously at it.

"But don't you think it would sound better
like this?" Sunny said.

She put her hind legs up on the oak tree and
built a beat around the lyrics with her hooves.

"Sheep…"

Drumma-drumma—

"Are Nice,"

Drumma—"Baa!" *Drumma.*

"Sheep…"

Clippy-cloppy—

"Are Sweet,"

Drumma—"Baa-baa!"

Animal Antics

Sindy, Suzelle and Sadie looked down in surprise at their own hooves, which had started tapping halfway through the song.

"See?" Sunny said in triumph. "You DO like it my way!"

"It doesn't matter whether we like it or not," said Suzelle. "Serafina will never change it."

"Just sing the song the normal Woolly Farm way!" said Sindy.

"Huh!" said Sunny. She felt cross and disappointed. "And why should I do that? What's Woolly Farm ever done for me?"

"We're a flock," Sadie said. "We work together."

"But I'm just trying to cheer you all up!" Sunny shouted.

"The best way to cheer us up is to sing the song properly," said Suzelle.

And she trotted away, with Sadie and Sindy close behind.

That night, out in the field, Sunny found it hard to sleep. She lay awake, listening to the peaceful rumbling of the Woolly Farm flock as they snored around her.

"The three most important things in a sheep's life are farm, field and flock," her mother had said, before Sunny left Lively Farm for her new home. "Remember that, my dear, and you will be happy."

If the sheep of Woolly Farm didn't want fun,
there was nothing Sunny could do about it.
She would just have to make the best of things
– the Woolly Farm way.

It could be worse, Sunny thought bravely.
I could have been turned into lamb chops.
Instead, I've got fields, food – and the chance
to sing in a competition.

Over the next fortnight, Sunny did her best to be a Woolly Farm sort of sheep. She walked quietly. She waited for the other sheep to speak first. She kept her voice down. And at the end of each day, she went to a quiet corner of the field and danced all by herself until she was completely exhausted. It sort of helped.

"Much better, Sunny," said Serafina, as the choir sang through "Sheep Are Nice" for the hundredth time. "See what you can do when you put your mind to it? From the top, everyone! And – *Sheep ... Are ... Nice!*"

Sunny worked hard to sing the song the way Serafina and the others wanted her to. She had to do it the Woolly Farm way, or not at all.

Chapter Six

"You're very quiet, Sunny," said Suzelle, the day before the Haybury Fleece Fair.

"I'm doing my best," said Sunny dully.

"I'm sure you'll enjoy the competition," said Sindy. "Serafina's got everyone singing together really well now!"

Sunny sniffed unenthusiastically at the fresh crop of clover, which had sprung up in the corner of the top field. She'd taken herself off to dance extra hard after the two hundredth rehearsal of "Sheep Are Nice", and was totally tired out.

It's all about the competition, she reminded herself. *Farm, field and flock.*

"It's a shame we won't win," said Suzelle.

Sunny looked up. "What do you mean, we won't win?" she said. "We've got the same chance as everyone else, haven't we?"

The others started laughing. Sindy choked on her clover and had to spit it out.

"What's so funny?" Sunny said, bewildered.

"Didn't I tell you?" said Sadie, raising her voice over the giggles of the others. "The Haybury Farm flock always wins."

Sunny was shocked. "Why?" she asked. "Are they brilliant?"

"Not really," said Sadie. "But Balthasar

the Haybury Farm prize bull is the judge, and he always chooses the Haybury Farm flock. Simple."

Sunny felt like she had tripped over a tree root. She'd just had the most boring two weeks of her life behaving like the rest of the flock. She'd worked as hard as anything to get "Sheep Are Nice" sounding the way Serafina wanted it to. And it had all been for nothing?

"So why do we bother entering?" she demanded.

"Because we're there for the Haybury Herding Trophy anyway," said Sindy, recovering from her coughing fit.

"Besides, the Mudford Farm flock sound like a herd of pigs," Sadie added, "so we always beat *them*."

"*Pigs ... Are ... Nice ... oink, oink,*" Suzelle began singing, to the tune of "Sheep Are Nice".

Animal Antics

"*Pigs … Are … Pink. Pigs … Are … Fat … oink, oink…*" She stopped. "Can anyone think of something that rhymes with 'pink'?"

Stink, thought Sunny.

"Er – think?" said Sadie with a frown.

STINK, thought Sunny again.

"What about wink?" Sindy said.

"STINK, all right?" Sunny shouted, making the others jump out of their fleeces. "PIGS ALL STINK! AND SO DOES WOOLLY FARM!"

And she marched up the field to dance her hooves off for the second time that day.

"Time to practise for the Haybury Herding Trophy before we put you into the barn for the night," Dawson growled later that day. "I don't know why we bother. You're always terrible."

He herded the flock to a section of the top field where Farmer Woolly had laid out an area with straw bales and gates to practise in.

"Got your most beautiful singing voices with you, girls?" called Serafina. "Let's give this our best shot!"

"Yes, Serafina!" the flock called back.

"Yes, Serafina," said Sunny, through gritted teeth.

Things started going wrong straight away.

"Left!" Dawson shouted, as he drove Sunny and the others towards two sets of gates, one on the left and one on the right.

"Did he say left?" said Sadie.

"That's right," said Suzelle.

"Right?" said Sindy, looking worried. "Or left?"

Sunny was bumped and pushed this way and that as the flock milled around. Two gates fell over.

"Now, imagine that this is the Sheep Choir of the Year, and Balthasar the bull is watching," said Serafina, in the middle of all this. "This is the only rehearsal we'll get, walking and singing at the same time! After me. *Sheep ... Are...*"

"Right!" howled Dawson.

"*Sheep ... Are ... Right,*" sang the sheep in confusion.

"Is this right?" said Sadie, turning left.

"WRONG, turn RIGHT!" bellowed Dawson.

"*Sheep ... Grow ... Wool,*" the sheep sang

as they barged about, trying to keep their eyes on Serafina and the course, and their ears on Serafina and Dawson. *"Sheep … Go … Bleat."*

Halfway around the course, several sheep had turned left too many times. Some had turned right too few times. Half were back at the beginning, and only two had made it to the end. Much of the course had been demolished. The only good news was that the flock had reached the end of the song at the same time, thanks to Serafina's booming voice keeping them together.

Animal Antics

"I need a bone and a quiet lie-down," Dawson moaned.

Farmer Woolly ruffled the fur on Dawson's head. "Never mind, lad," he said, sensing the sheepdog's disappointment.

"Good singing, girls!" said Serafina. "Sing it that way and you'll do Woolly Farm proud!"

"Get your smelly sheep bums down the hill," Dawson said to the flock despairingly.

The flock galloped down from the top field into the farmyard, bumping Sunny from side to side. Everyone was in a good mood thanks to Serafina's words of praise, and were bleating and shoving and singing snatches of "Sheep Are Nice" as they went.

Sunny just wanted to cry.

"Last year we flattened the judging bench as well as the gates," Suzelle told Sunny, as the sheep jostled into the barn for the night.

"Singing and following instructions at the same time is really hard," Sindy sighed.

"But at least we'll do the singing bit OK," said Sadie brightly. "Thanks to Serafina!"

"You'll all be marvellous," said Sir Simon from his pen. His polished horns gleamed in the dim light of the barn. "Or should I say *ewe'll*. Ha ha!"

"The flock is in fine voice tonight," Mrs Woolly said to her husband, as they locked the barn doors. "Anyone would think they were having a choir practice."

"Right funny choir that would be," said Farmer Woolly.

And they went into the farmhouse for their supper.

Chapter seven

The day of the Haybury Fleece Fair dawned
warm and sunny.

"Do Woolly Farm proud, ladies!" Sir Simon
called, as one of Farmer Woolly's farmhands
loaded him up for the Rutley Ram Regatta.
"I love you all. Or should I say *ewe*. Ha ha!"

"You too, Sir Simon!" called the flock, as the
ram's trailer door closed behind him and Sir

Simon trundled out of the farmyard and on to Woolly Farm Lane.

"Get on, then," said Farmer Woolly gently, tapping at the nearest sheep bottom.

Dawson snapped at Sunny's feet, making her jump. "Get into the truck, you imbeciles," he growled. "One foot in front of the other. And try not to knock each other off the ramp."

"As if we'd knock each other off the ramp," Sindy said, as they bundled into the truck that would take them to Haybury Farm. "What does he think we are – stupid?"

"Of course I think you're stupid," came Dawson's voice behind them. "You're sheep."

There was a clattering noise behind them. Over the tops of all the woolly backs, Sunny caught sight of Serafina. The old sheep was lying on her back at the bottom of the ramp, bleating in pain.

"Oh no!" said Suzelle in dismay. "Someone just knocked Serafina off the ramp!"

Farmer Woolly and two other farmhands rushed to examine Serafina. Sunny could hear anxious muttering on all sides.

"Is Serafina OK?"

"Is she still coming?"

"Don't worry, girls!" Serafina called, struggling to get back on to her feet and falling down again. "I'll be with you in a tick…"

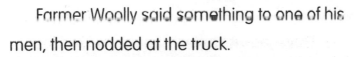

Farmer Woolly said something to one of his men, then nodded at the truck.

"What's Farmer Woolly saying, Dawson?" Sunny asked the sheepdog, who was watching, his black ears pricked and alert.

"He's not bringing her," said Dawson.

There was a gasp of horror from the flock.

"But that means we can't enter Sheep Choir of the Year!" wailed Sadie.

"Tough luck," Dawson said. "Time to shut the truck. I'll see you at Haybury Farm. And if you embarrass me in the Haybury Herding Trophy this year, I'll eat every last one of you."

"What's got into the sheep?" said Farmer Woolly to his wife, as they turned in through the gates of Haybury Farm after a bumpy couple of hours. "They've been bleating up a storm ever since we left!"

"They probably don't like your driving," said Mrs Woolly. She stroked Dawson's ears as he lay on the seat beside her.

But it wasn't Farmer Woolly's driving that was bothering the flock. In the back of the van, the sheep had other things to worry about.

"But we can't enter Sheep Choir of the Year without Serafina!" Sadie wailed for the hundredth time. "We've never practised without her. We don't know what to do!"

"We know the words backwards, Sadie," Sunny said, doing her best to sound encouraging. "Nice … Are … Sheep. See? Just because we don't have Serafina to keep our singing together, it doesn't mean we can't do it."

Sadie looked even more horrified. "Nice … Are … Sheep?" she said. "I thought it was Sheep … Are … Nice!"

"Now I'm confused," said Sindy.

Several other sheep started muttering, making Sunny wish she hadn't said anything at all. Once again, Sadie wailed, "We can't enter without Serafina. We just CAN'T!"

The truck shuddered to a stop. The bright spring sunshine poured through the back door as the ramp was lowered, making Sunny blink.

"Out you get," Dawson said. He looked depressed. "Two hours before you lot flatten everything I drive you through."

The Woolly Farm sheep bustled down the ramp and into a pen. Sunny looked around. It was impossible not to feel excited. There were people and sheep everywhere. Big white tents billowed, red and blue and yellow bunting fluttering like petals in the wind, and human voices boomed through a loudspeaker above the Woolly Farm pen. In the field in front

Animal Antics

of the pen, an area was marked out with bales and fencing, ready for the herding event.

In the neighbouring field, an enormous chestnut-coloured bull gazed over the five-bar gate with a bored look on his face. The brass ring in his nose gleamed in the sunshine.

"Is that Balthasar?" Sunny asked Suzelle.

Suzelle nodded. "Big, isn't he?"

Balthasar was *huge*. He chewed mouthfuls of grass and watched the scene through half-open eyes. Every now and then he gave a yawn.

Animal Antics

A flock of haughty-looking black-faced sheep were practising "Sheep Are Nice" two pens down. Their voices were strong, but they weren't singing together. They sounded like this:

"*SheepSheepSheep … AreAreAre … NiceNiceNice…*"

"They're not very good," said Sunny.

"That's the Haybury Farm flock," said Suzelle. "They could sing like turnips and they'd still win."

"Talking of turnips," Sindy said, "listen to the Mudford lot."

Sunny heard the most terrible noise drifting on the wind. "That's *singing*?" she said, peering at the chunky white Mudford Farm sheep, who were trotting towards a large shed not too far away.

"Apparently, yes," said Suzelle. "Now, we've got the shearing to look forward to. I'm totally boiling in this fleece!"

Chapter Eight

Sunny had never been shorn before. Although her coat wasn't as thick as Suzelle's, it was thick enough to be uncomfortable in the spring sunshine.

"Don't wriggle or they'll shear off your ears by mistake," Suzelle advised, as Dawson herded them all to the shearing shed.

Sunny gulped.

"And if they turn you upside down, let them," Suzelle added. "It's undignified and uncomfortable. But it feels fantastic afterwards."

The Mudford Farm sheep came trotting out of the shearing shed ahead of the Woolly Farm flock, freshly shorn and singing worse than ever.

"*SHeep*," they screeched, "*ArE. NiCe. ShEeP. ARe…*"

"All right, Dawson?" said Detmar, Mudford Farm's fat and cheerful German Shepherd. "Looking forward to your herding performance. I'll stand back though, eh?"

"Ha ha, Detmar," said Dawson glumly.

The shearing shed was hot and dark and full of sweaty humans waving shears. A long arm reached out and grabbed Sunny. Moments later, she felt the cold metal blades snickering over her back, head and bottom, then she was turned upside down and given the same treatment on her belly. Before Sunny knew it, she was back on her feet. The spring breeze on her closely-trimmed body was lovely. She felt as light as a feather. It was WONDERFUL.

All Sunny's old energy came flooding back. "Whoopee!" she shouted, with a huge kick and a jump.

"Good, isn't it?" said a skinny-looking sheep with a familiar face.

"Suzelle?" Sunny gasped.

Everyone looked so different, it was hard to tell who was who. Sindy looked especially happy. It turned out she was bigger than Suzelle without her fleece on.

Animal Antics

"Stop admiring each other and concentrate," Dawson growled. "The pen is that way. THAT WAY!"

"Got any sheep this year, Dawson?" called the pretty-looking border collie herding the newly-shorn Haybury Farm flock back to their pen. "Or are they still a bunch of goats?"

Sunny felt cross at being called a goat. "We're going to win this year!" she shouted.

JUST WATCH US!

"Hi, Dusty," Dawson muttered.

"I like your new goat, Dawson," Dusty spluttered, as the Haybury Farm flock howled with laughter. "She's hilarious!" And she herded her flock onwards with a jaunty wave of her plumy tail.

"You shouldn't have said that stuff about winning, Sunny," Sindy groaned.

Perhaps it was the fact that Serafina wasn't there. Or maybe it was because the whole flock looked so miserable and scared that Sunny knew she had to do something about it. Or maybe it was just the loveliness of the warm air on her shorn skin. But whatever it was, Sunny knew she was back to her old self – whether the Woolly Farm flock liked it or not.

"I meant it," Sunny said, holding her head up high. "We can win Sheep Choir of the Year *and* the Haybury Herding Trophy."

The flock scoffed. The two old ewes, Sue and Sandra, shook their heads sadly.

"We can't do herding!"

"We can't sing without Serafina leading us!"

Sunny listened to the other flocks practising "Sheep Are Nice" up and down the field. Woolly Farm could be the best. She knew it.

"We can do it if we work together," she said. "See how bored Balthasar looks? We can blow the ring out of that big bull's nose!"

Balthasar gazed glassily over the gate, chewing slowly on his grass.

"Aren't you listening?" Sindy said. "We haven't got Serafina!"

"Even Mudford Farm will beat us this year!" said Sue, the whiskers in her nose quivering with distress.

"We simply can't enter without Serafina!" Sadie wailed.

"I could teach you how to bleat-box!" Sunny said, refusing to give up. "Balthasar will have to give us extra points if we do that."

"Learn all those silly rhythms you were doing back in the top field?" said Sandra in horror. "What would Serafina say?"

"Serafina!" sighed Sadie, shaking her head in despair.

"Well, how about if I do a bleat-boxing solo over the top?" Sunny suggested.

The flock looked more frightened than ever.

"But we can't even sing in time without Serafina," said Suzelle. "A solo over the top would confuse us even more. Don't be such a donkey, Sunny!"

Sunny lost her patience. "First I'm a goat and now I'm a donkey," she shouted. "And you lot call yourself sheep, I suppose? You're acting like a bunch of carrots! I've learned a lot about working together since I came to Woolly Farm, and I know this. We can DO stuff if we work as a team. Farm, field and flock!"

It was a heroic speech. But it didn't work. The Woolly Farm sheep turned their shorn backs on Sunny and gathered in the far corner of the pen to mutter amongst themselves.

Chapter Nine

The Sheep Choir of the Year (and the Haybury
Herding Trophy) began at exactly three o'clock.
Sunny stood on her own at the front of the
Woolly Farm pen. The other sheep were still
standing in the far corner, bleating together in
low voices. Sunny was sure they were saying
nasty things about her.

The first five choirs performed "Sheep Are

Nice" while making their way around the
course. Most of them knocked over the fences,
or sang all the wrong notes, or both. As far as
Sunny could tell, the course and the song were
both quite easy. The problem was doing them
at the same time. Even if Serafina had been
there to lead them, that particular problem
was not going to go away.

All the fresh energy Sunny had felt since
losing her thick fleece was leaking away.
Suzelle, Sadie, Sindy and the others were right.
It was stupid trying to come up with an answer

Animal Antics

to such an impossible problem.

Next up was the Mudford Farm Flock.
"*SHeeP. MaKE. WoOl,*" they shrieked, as Detmar
the German Shepherd herded them around the
course at full speed. "*ShEEp. GO. BleAt.*"

Suzelle's voice made Sunny jump.

"The Mudford Farm sheep might sound like
Farmer Woolly's tractor, but they sure know
how to move."

Sunny looked round. The whole of the
Woolly Farm flock had come to the front of the
pen again and were looking – sheepish.

"SHeeP. ArE. NICe!" croaked the Mudford sheep, trotting through the last fence. They'd only knocked one gate out of place.

"Yeah, they're quite good," Sunny said after a minute.

"Are you OK?" Suzelle said.

"What do you care," Sunny muttered.

"Don't give up on us, Sunny," Sadie replied. "Please?"

Sunny blinked.

"We've talked about it and we think you're right about working together," Sindy added. "Let's face it. What have we got to lose?"

Both Sue and Sandra said, "Farm, field and flock!" in a bold, un-Woolly Farm sort of way.

"Boo-boo, baa-boo!" added Sue, with a creaky sort of bottom wiggle. Sandra looked at her elderly friend in astonishment.

"So," said Sindy in a hopeful voice. "Got any

bright ideas, Sunny? We need all the help we can get."

Before Sunny could break the news that she had no ideas at all, Dawson put his nose through the pen.

"We're on after the Haybury lot," he said. "Time to switch on that brain cell of yours. I know you've only got one and you need time to warm it up."

Animal Antics

Dusty the Haybury Farm collie winked at Dawson as she trotted into the arena with her flock. The field fell quiet. The loudspeaker shouted something. And the Haybury Farm flock was off.

Dusty herded them around the first corner, her tail waving merrily as they sang the opening notes of "Sheep Are Nice". Balthasar the prize bull watched sleepily from his field.

"Please tell us you've had an idea, Sunny," Suzelle begged.

Sunny was concentrating on Dusty. The collie's tail steadily waved from side to side as the flock sang and moved through the course. "Sheep Are Nice" was all over the place.

"SheepSheepSheep…"

Wag wag…

"AreAreAre … AllAllAll…"

Wag wag…

"QuietQuietQuiet…"

Wag wag…

"AsAsAs … MiceMiceMice…"

Suddenly, Sunny had a wonderful idea.
A fantastic idea. An UTTERLY BRILLIANT IDEA.
She nudged Suzelle.

"Look at Dusty's tail!" she gasped.

"She's wagging it," Suzelle said.

"Dogs do that," said Sindy.

"The flock isn't singing together," said
Sunny. She was so excited, she could hardly
get her words out. "But
Dusty's wagging her
tail in perfect
time!"

The flock
gazed at Sunny
like she was
talking human.

"Don't you GET it?" said Sunny. "When we sing, we follow Serafina's voice to keep us together. But as we don't have Serafina to follow today, we can watch Dawson's tail instead! Wag, wag. Wag, wag. Follow his tail and we'll all sing in time!"

"It's not working for the Haybury Farm flock," said Sindy.

"That's because Dusty's behind them," said Sunny.

"But Dawson's always behind *us*," Sindy pointed out. "We won't see his tail either."

"I've thought of that," Sunny said. "If we want to win Sheep Choir of the Year and have a chance at the Haybury Herding Trophy too, then I have a plan. It's going to sound crazy, but trust me – it'll work. We need to persuade Dawson…" She glanced over at the sheepdog. "But once we've done that, it's in the bag! Listen up…"

Chapter Ten

"You want to do WHAT?" said Dawson, when Sunny told him the plan.

"Walk backwards around the course," repeated Sunny. "We can follow your tail that way. And we can probably listen better too, because we'll be able to see you."

"But you won't be able to see the gates!" said Dawson helplessly.

"Seeing the gates never helps, to be honest," said Suzelle.

"Oh, and because we'll be looking at you, our left and your left won't be the same," Sunny added. "Remember to say 'left' if you want us to turn to your right. And maybe point with your nose while you're at it."

A big cheer went up. The Haybury Farm flock had finished the course, with two gates out of place and one sheep still singing *"Sheep … Are … Great…"*

"You're serious?" the collie said. "You'd trust me to get you through the gates without actually seeing them?"

"Yes," said Sunny. "Provided you wag your tail."

Dawson was too stunned for his usual insults. Instead he looked at his tail. "I don't wag it much," he said.

"Well, now's the time to try," said Sunny.

The rest of the flock bleated in agreement. Dawson's tail started to twitch.

"That's it!" said Suzelle. "You're doing it, Dawson."

"Lovely, Dawson," Sunny said in her most flattering voice.

Dawson's tail wagged a bit harder. He looked at it in amazement.

"I suppose it can't be any worse than last year," he said. "And if it works, the crowd…"

"Will go crazy," Sindy said.

"Imagine how much Dusly would admire you," Sunny added. "Driving your flock backwards around the course! Such control! Such brilliance!"

Animal Antics

"Right," Dawson said. His chest swelled and his tail went faster. "Right…"

The loudspeaker crackled above their heads.

"Get on then," said Farmer Woolly, unhooking the pen and tapping Sandra on the bottom.

"Our turn, ladies," said Dawson. His tail was now sweeping from side to side like a stem of black and white barley in a breeze. "Do your worst."

Animal Antics

The crowd started muttering in surprise as the Woolly Farm flock gathered in front of Dawson, their rumps pointing at the first gate.

Dawson cleared his throat. "Left," he said. "I mean, right. Right!"

His tail was slowing down with nerves. He pointed his nose the way he wanted the flock to go.

"*Sheep…*" began the Woolly Farm flock very slowly, backing away to Dawson's left. "*Are … Nice…*"

"Er, yeah, that's good," Dawson said, as they reversed through the first gate with no trouble at all. His tail picked up a little speed. "Now straight back for a bit. That's it... That's it..."

"Sheep ... Are ... Sweet..."

The flock's voices rang out clear and true, cutting through the amazed laughter of the crowd.

"Right!" shouted Dawson. "Back a bit more... Sharp left! You're doing it! By all the bones in Belgium, you're doing it!"

"Sheep ... Grow ... Wool," sang the flock, speeding up again as Dawson's tail got faster.

Sunny couldn't help it. "Sheep are cool, yeah!" she bleat-boxed, tapping her hooves.

The rest of the flock kept singing, watching Dawson's tail as it wagged back and forth.

"Sheep ... Go ... Bleat..."

Animal Antics

"Sheep rule, yeah!" Sunny bleat-boxed, adding another flourish with her hooves.

"*Sheep…*"

"Rock the field!"

"*Are … All…*"

"Rock the barn, yo!"

"*Quiet…*"

"So quiet!"

"*As … Mice…*"

"To be precise, yeah!"

And then Sunny couldn't fit in any more bleat-boxing because the flock sang the last lines of the song too fast, thanks to the whirl that was Dawson's tail.

"*SheepAreGreatSheepAreNiiice!*"

The Woolly Farm sheep made it through the final gate just as they sang the last note. They'd done it without knocking over a single thing. The crowd went bonkers. They'd never seen anything like it.

"Look at Balthasar!" shouted Suzelle. "He dropped a whole mouthful of grass! I've never seen him do that before!"

All the other sheep (apart from the Haybury Farm flock) crowded up to the edges of their pens, bleating and drumming their hooves. Detmar the German Shepherd looked annoyed. Dusty's mouth hung open almost as wide as Balthasar's.

Animal Antics

"I never thought I'd say this, but I love sheep," Dawson said, as Farmer Woolly rubbed his head so hard it made the sheepdog's voice shake. "I love yoo-hoo-hoo aw-aw-all."

Sunny grinned. "Or should that be…"

"EWE!" shouted the Woolly Farm sheep. "Farm, field and flock for ever! Farm, field and flock!"

Animal Antics

Woolly Farm won the Haybury Herding Trophy to storms of applause from the crowd. The flock watched happily as Farmer Woolly and Dawson strode up to the podium to collect the prize. Dawson's tail was a blur.

"What do you call sheep that live together?" Sandra asked suddenly.

The other sheep looked surprised by the question.

"Sheep mates?" Sue guessed.

"Pen friends."

"Pen what?" said Sue.

"Forget it," said Sandra. "What do you call a sheep with no legs?"

"Unhappy," said Sue.

"A cloud," said Sandra patiently. "Get it? No legs?"

Animal Antics

Sue gave a funny honking laugh.

"You-hoo-hoo sound like a goo-hoo-hoose when you laugh!" Sandra giggled.

"You-hoo-hoo sound like a HOR-HOR-HORSE!" guffawed Sue.

And the two old sheep laughed so hard they had to lean against the side of the pen for support.

Sunny grinned as everyone around the pen caught Sue and Sandra's giggles. She had a feeling life on Woolly Farm was about to get a lot more fun.

Just a bit left...

"I would like to say," bellowed Balthasar the Haybury Farm prize bull, "that in all my years of judging Sheep Choir of the Year, I've never heard a flock of sheep sing as well as our last performers. I could hear every word. You were together. You were in tune. You actually made my hooves tap. AND you were moving backwards throughout. So, I'm proud and a little confused to say that the title of Sheep Choir of the Year goes to – Woolly Farm."

As the cheers erupted from the Woolly Farm pen, Balthasar looked at his own flock of sheep.

"Sorry," he said. "But you lot were rubbish."

"Don't worry about it, Balthasar," Dusty said. "Now, I simply must go and give Dawson a good sniff."

And a bit more...

"I've never heard that bull bellow so loud before," said Farmer Woolly, proudly cradling the Haybury Herding Trophy under one arm and resting his other hand on Dawson's neck. "Sounded like he was making a speech."

"I think he enjoyed the show," said Mrs Woolly. "So did the sheep, by all accounts. They look like they're celebrating."

"You say the daftest things, wife," Farmer Woolly laughed.

Totally True

New Zealand sheep farmers have to pay a special tax because sheep farts damage the ozone layer.

FARP

Dogs have twice as many muscles to move their ears as people.

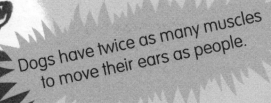

You can lead a bull upstairs ... but you can't lead it down again.

Border collies are the cleverest dog breed in the world, together with golden retrievers – and poodles.

Sheep only have teeth in their lower jaws.

If a sheep falls on its back, it can't get up again.

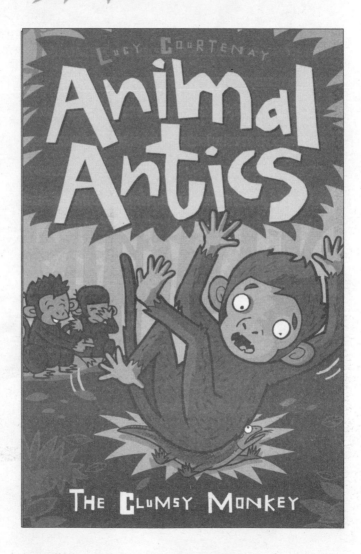

LUCY COURTENAY

Animal Antics

THE CLUMSY MONKEY